This ELMER book belongs to:

. . . .

For Angelo and Laura

This American edition published in 2012 for Books are Fun by Andersen Press Ltd.,
20 Vauxhall Bridge Road, London SW1V 2SA.
Text and Illustration copyright © David McKee, 1991
The rights of David McKee to be identified as the author and illustrator
of this work have been asserted by him in accordance with
the Copyright, Designs and Patents Act, 1988.
All rights reserved.
British Library Cataloguing in Publication Data available.

Color separated in Switzerland by Photolitho AG, Zürich.
Manufactured in China by C & C Offset Printing Co., Ltd.
1-C&C-6/26/12

ISBN 978 1 84939 551 9

ELMER
AGAIN

David McKee

Andersen Press

Elmer, the patchwork elephant, was bored. It was two days before another Elmer's day parade – the day when elephants cover themselves with bright patterns. The colors were ready and the elephants were quietly thinking about how they would decorate themselves.

Elmer didn't have to think. He was always colored gray for the parade, the only gray elephant.

"Time for a walk," he said to himself.

As he walked Elmer thought,
"It's too quiet around here. We need a
joke or something to liven things up."
He came to a pool and looked at his reflection.
"Hello, Elmer," he said to himself in the water.
"You've just given me a good idea. Thank you."

When he returned the others were still quietly thinking. Elmer went up to one of them and whispered in his ear. The other elephant smiled and winked but said nothing. Elmer settled down for a rest. He had a long night in front of him.

When night fell Elmer waited until the others were asleep.
Then, taking care not to wake them, he set to work.

Before sunrise he had finished and he tiptoed off to another part of the forest to sleep for what was left of the night.

In the morning the first elephant to wake looked at his neighbour and said, "Good morning Elmer." One after another the elephants woke, and as they did, from every direction came,
"Good morning, Elmer,"
"GOOD morning, Elmer,"
"Good MORNING, Elmer,"
"GOOD MORNING, Elmer,"
"Good morning, ELMER," and so on.

During the night Elmer had painted all the elephants to look like him. Now there were Elmers everywhere and nobody knew which was the real one.

Then the elephants started to speak to each other and say things like, "Are you Elmer?"

"I don't know," the other might say. "I might be today, but I'm sure I wasn't yesterday."

Then, one of the elephants called out, "This is another Elmer trick. Come on. Let's splash across the river and wash off the colors. Then we'll see who the real Elmer is."

The elephants raced to the river and splashed and sploshed their way to the other side.

Once on the other side the elephants stared. They were *all* gray.

"Where's Elmer?" they asked.

"Here of course," said a gray elephant. "Don't you recognize me?"

"But you're the same color as us," gasped the others.

"So I am," said Elmer. "Wonderful. I always wanted to be like you."

"This is awful," said another elephant. "Elmer can't be like the rest of us. Things won't be the same without an Elmer."

"Well there's nothing I can do about it," said Elmer, "unless . . ."

"What?" said the others.

"Well," said Elmer, "the colors that washed off are still floating on the water. Perhaps if I run back through them I may return to normal."

"Try it," shouted the others. "Try anything to get your colors back."

"Yahoo!" called Elmer, and he raced across the river and vanished into the trees on the other side.

Almost at once he reappeared puffing and panting, but once again in his bright patchwork colors.
"Hooray!" cheered the elephants from across the river.
"It worked. We've got our Elmer again." With that the elephants started chanting, "ELMER, ELMER, ELMER."

Beside Elmer another elephant suddenly appeared from out of the trees. "Did you call?" he asked. The other elephants went silent and stared. This other elephant was soaking wet as if he had just run across the river. On top of that both Elmer and the other elephant were laughing.

"You tricked us," said one elephant to the wet, gray elephant. "You were working with Elmer and pretended to be him. We should have known Elmer's colors wouldn't wash off. It's another Elmer trick."

With that the whole herd of elephants burst out laughing, and running back into the river they started to splash the two Elmers and each other and once again they chanted,

"ELMER, ELMER, ELMER," until the whole jungle shook with their noisy game.

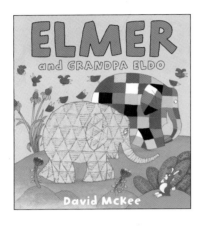 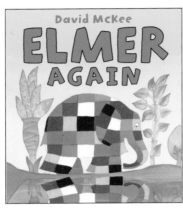 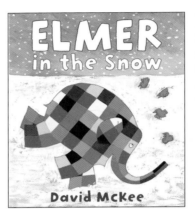 

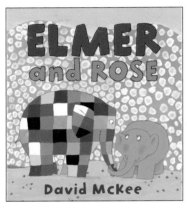  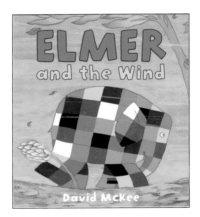 

Enjoy more Elmer stories from:

www.andersenpressusa.com

www.lernerbooks.com

www.oceanhousemedia.com